The Great Pirate Christmas Battle

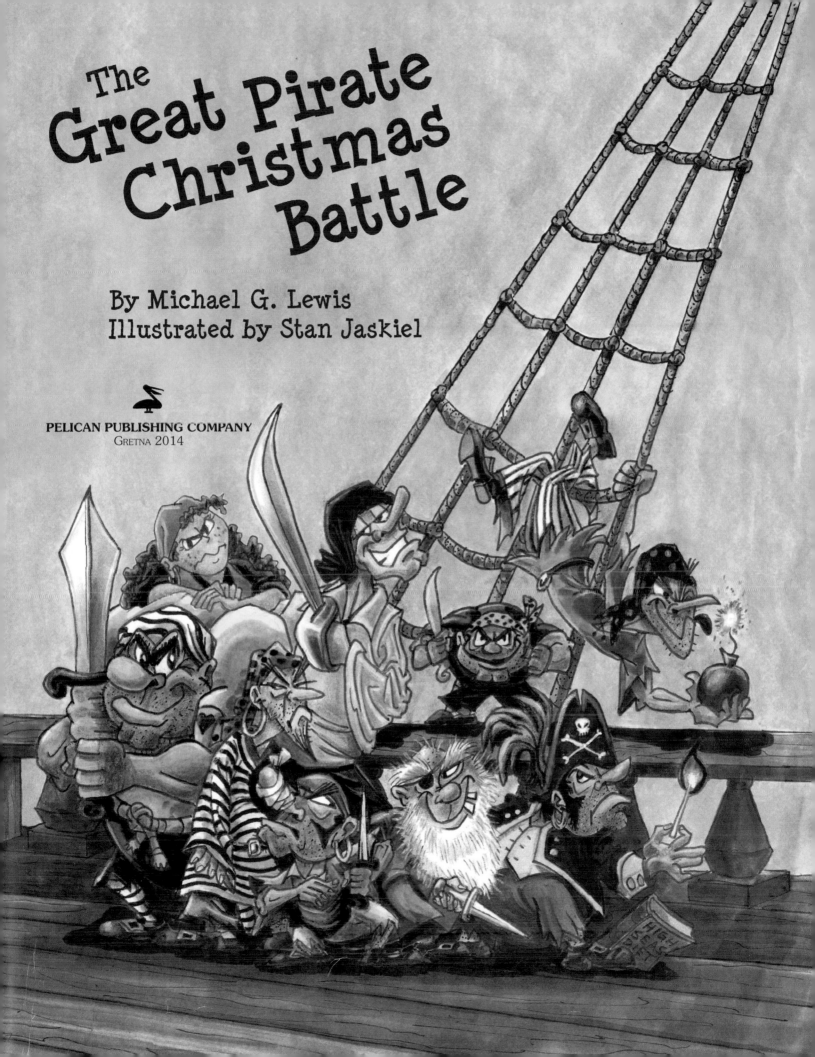

The Great Pirate Christmas Battle

By Michael G. Lewis
Illustrated by Stan Jaskiel

PELICAN PUBLISHING COMPANY
GRETNA 2014

To my parents, Mim and John. And to my treasured crew: Elaine, Aidan, Brady, Owen, and Garrett.—M. L.

To Judy, who keeps our ship on course. And to my dad, who taught me to draw.—S. J.

The word "Pelican" and the depiction of a pelican are trademarks of Pelican Publishing Company, Inc., and are registered in the U.S. Patent and Trademark Office.

Library of Congress Cataloging-in-Publication Data

Lewis, Michael (Michael G.), 1961-
   The great pirate Christmas battle / by Michael Lewis ; illustrated by Stan Jaskiel.
      pages cm
   Summary: Illustrations and rhyming text tell of Cap'n McNasty, who leads his pirate crew in stealing—and playing with—Christmas toys until Santa himself arrives to teach them a lesson.
   ISBN 978-1-4556-1934-4 (hardcover : alk. paper) — ISBN 978-1-4556-1935-1 (e-book) [1. Stories in rhyme. 2. Pirates—Fiction. 3. Stealing—Fiction. 4. Toys—Fiction. 5. Santa Claus—Fiction.] I. Jaskiel, Stan, illustrator. II. Title.
   PZ8.3.L5912Gre 2014
   [E]—dc23
                                                        2014001403

Printed in Malaysia

Published by Pelican Publishing Company, Inc.
1000 Burmaster Street, Gretna, Louisiana 70053

Me name is Cap'n McNasty, an' I owned all the seas with me fearless pirate crew, doin' as we please!

Arrr, no one dared stop us, mate—
nay, not even a whale!
But to an end it did come,
so listen to me tale.

One Christmas Eve I had a plan:
we would sail about
a-stealin' all the presents
ol' Santa had left out!

Back to the ship we headed
to find out what we'd got.
Nasty pirates, yes we wuz,
with booty worth a lot!

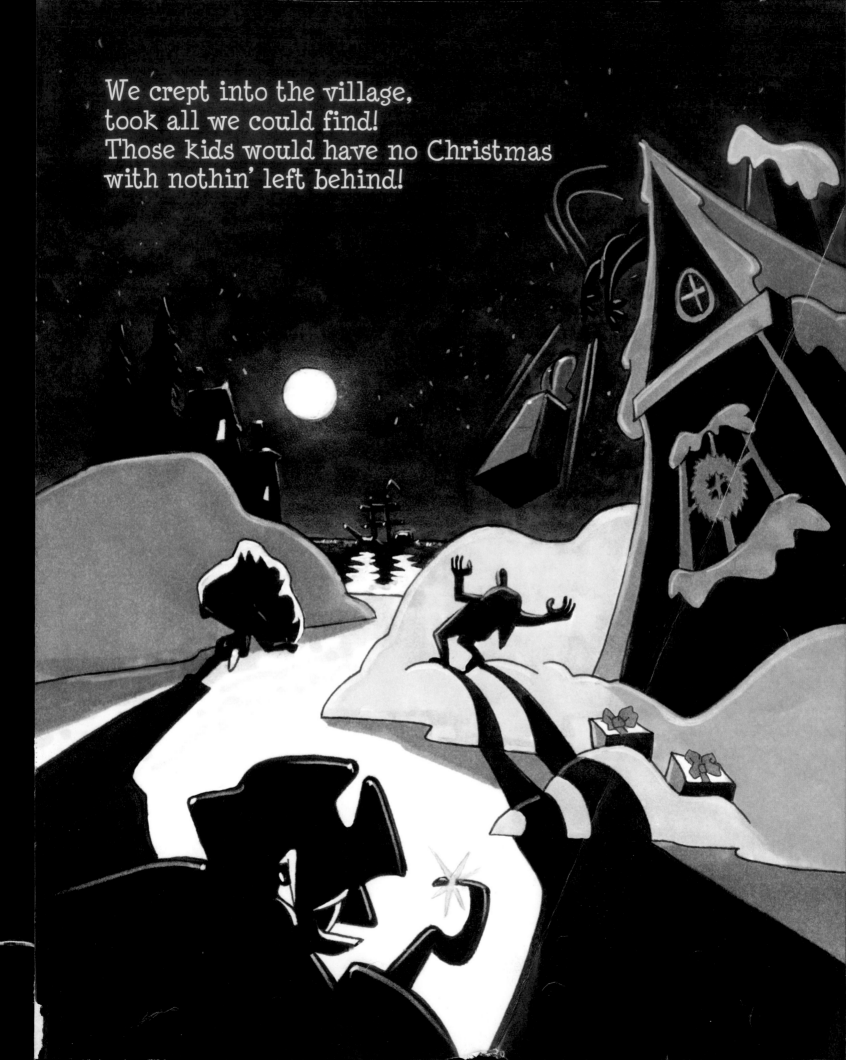

We crept into the village,
took all we could find!
Those kids would have no Christmas
with nothin' left behind!

The toys—better than treasure!
Yo ho ho! Such fun!
Stinky Mick on a pogo stick
and me with a pop gun!

There wuz cupcakes and cookies
and pies of all kind.
We played with puzzles and games
and tops that you wind!

I gathered round me scallywags
sayin', "Listen here!
There ain't no one to stop us . . .
We'll do this every year!"

Then high from up the lookout nest,
Black Bart, he did scream,
"If I ain't gone bonkers, Cap,
Maybe it's a dream—"

Run I did, across the deck,
a-spyin' on the swells:
Santa on a bright, red ship,
singin' "Jingle Bells!"

He had several tiny mates
workin' as his crew
and a herd o' magic deer—
'cross the sky they flew!

As they pulled his bright, red ship
quick across the sea,
Santa wuz a-ho ho ho-in',
headin' straight for me!

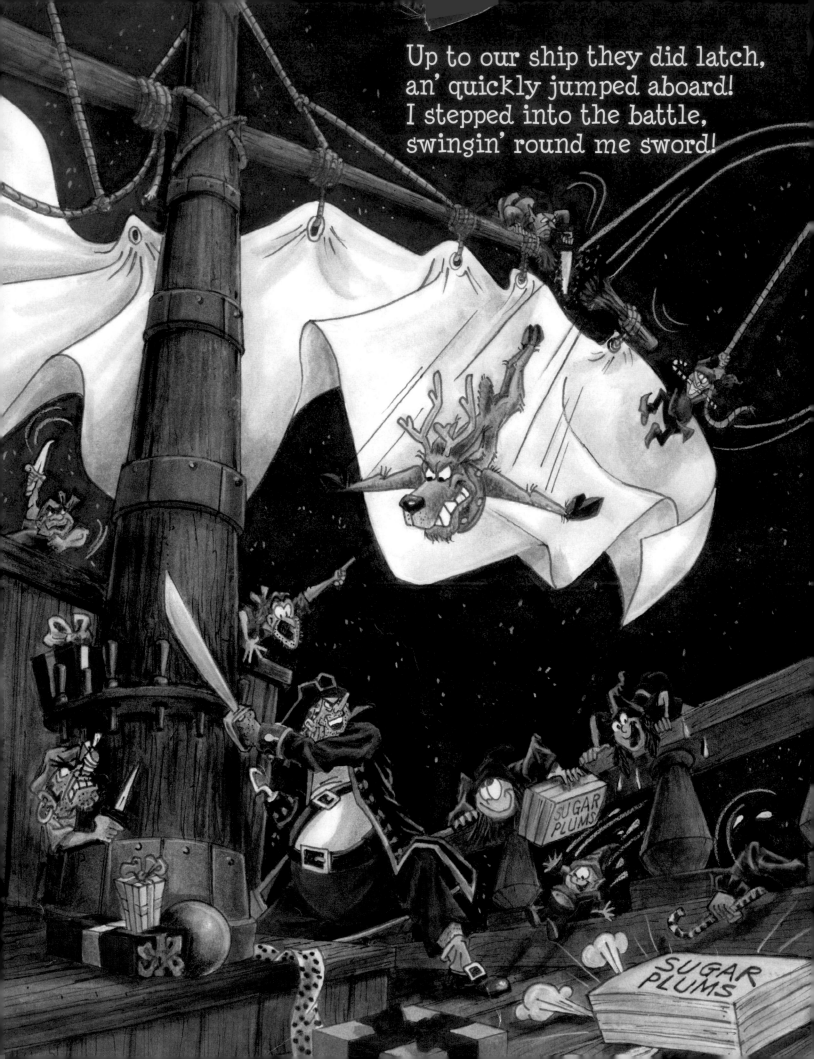

Up to our ship they did latch,
an' quickly jumped aboard!
I stepped into the battle,
swingin' round me sword!

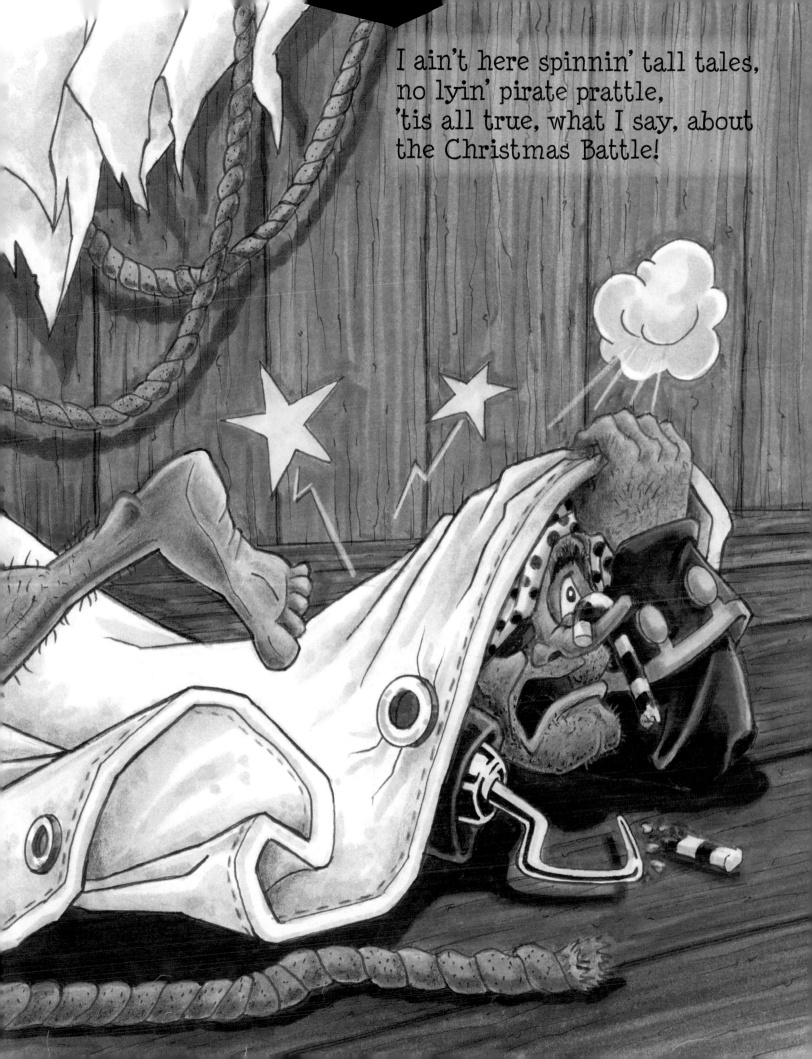

Poutin' Pam and several more
had nowhere to go
a-tied up to the mainsail
in a Christmas bow!

One-Eye Will and Too Tall Tim
never had a chance;
those pesky elves took fruitcake
and stuffed it in their pants.

All the others done fell down
(landed on their bums!),
from slippin' and a slidin'
on crates of sugar plums!

They showed no hesitatin'
nor a hint o' fear;
overrun with elves were we,
and flyin' reindeer!

Old St. Nick squared off with me,
the last to remain.
I pulled out me nasty hook,
and he, a candy cane.

Avast, it didn't last long—
now use yer 'maginations.
He covered me in bright lights
and Christmas decorations!

Well, blow me down, they beat us!
Aye, they did, no doubt!
As they quickly sailed away,
Santa turned to shout:

"I hope you learned your lesson
and won't be stealing toys
that I leave around the world
for all the girls and boys!"

Off they went with everything—
well, that ain't quite true.
When Santa did his headcount,
his ship wuz short a crew.

Ye know, I am a pirate,
just can't help meself.
When Santa weren't a-lookin' . . .